GABE

UNDERCOVER LOVER SERIES — BOOK II

Cover Design by: Bella Media Management

GABE

UNDERCOVER LOVER SERIES — BOOK II

C. A. SALO

CHAPTER 1

"GABRIEL, STOP IT!" TAMARA YELLED.

Gabe slammed the side of his body against the thick metal door.

Her body shaky with adrenaline as she saw the huge man before her kicking the door with power.

"Gabe, Gabe, stop, please," she pleaded, her voice weak, her throat burning with the sobs rising.

She watched him stop, his chest heaving with labored breaths as he turned to her. "Please stop before you hurt yourself."

"We'll both be dead if we don't get the hell out of here."

His snarl bore deep down to her bones. She knew it wasn't aimed at her, but the psycho who'd locked them in. "I know." Her chest rose unsteadily as she calmed the anxiety blanketing her senses, focusing on not letting the panic control her.

"It's my job to protect you," he growled, pacing the confines of the small storage room they'd been tossed into.

"You can't protect me if you hurt yourself."

"I couldn't protect you from getting locked in here!"

"You protected me from getting killed!" She screamed back as he whipped around, the anger in his eyes apparent as they met hers. "If it wasn't for you, I'd be dead." Her voice cracked as she stepped to him, laying her hand over the damp t-shirt covering his muscled chest. "I'd be dead," she whispered, her head resting against his chest as his arms wrapped around her trembling body, drawing her to him, his cheek lying on the top of her head, using his nearness to fight the fright within, inhaling his masculine scent as her tears wet his shirt.

"It's all right, Tamara," his voice was soft as he held her close. "I won't let him hurt you."

She knew he'd put himself in front of her again to protect her, and heard her inner voice screaming for him to do it, because she was more than a job.

She'd walked into a small mom and pop store to buy a quick dinner for the night and ended up right in the middle of a robbery-homicide. If Detective Gabriel Mac Cloud hadn't been coming in right behind her when she'd startled the guy, his bullet would have gone right through her. "Because it's your job, Gabe, or something else?" she mumbled against his shoulder, the twitch of his muscles clear against her cheek, before he nudged her chin up with a finger.

Gabe smiled when he met her gaze. "I think you know the answer to that counselor." Lowering his head, his lips touched hers softly, gently, hesitantly. The first kiss always a tender and unsure move.

Tamara sighed, her head tilted, granting him better access as she deepened the kiss. Her tongue stroked his bottom lip before slipping slowly between his. Honestly, she'd wanted to do this forever. He extruded such alpha tendencies, just like his brothers, but him, Gabriel Mac Cloud sent her vaginal muscles clenching every time she caught sight of him, and that had scared the shit out of her.

So, she'd pushed him away for two years, always keeping an arm's length between them, until recently. Until they'd been forced to work together on a case with his brother, and her secretary. "Gabe," she whispered as she leaned back, her eyes fluttered, and her tongue dipped out to lick her lower lip and his essence off. "I, um, I don't know if this is the right time." Meeting his gaze, she liked the fact he'd let her control the kiss.

Gabe shrugged. "Probably not." Drawing her into his embrace, he laid his cheek on top of her head. "But ask me if I give a shit right now."

"What are we going to do?"

"I don't know."

Tamara gasped as she pulled back. "I have my cell, it wasn't in my purse when he took it," she whispered, watching as he lowered his eyes to hers. Working quickly, she grabbed the small inch-thick device out of her pocket and put it on silent. "There's no bars." Stepping away, she moved around the room trying to get the bars on her phone to go up.

"It's the room, Tam, it's blocking the reception."

Tamara's fears lessened when she sensed his presence behind her. Her eyes flew up to his when he grabbed the phone out of her hand. Her head whipped to the door and gasped when the lock turned.

Gabe shoved the phone into his back pocket. "Stay behind me, no matter what happens."

"Gabe…"

"Do it," he growled.

When she saw the fierceness in his gaze she didn't know what else to do but nod, her eyes slowly lowering to the door as it opened. The guy holding them was definitely on some sort of drug; he was jumpy, edgy, wired. Anyway, you described it, that's what he was. Her stomach clenched with fear when his eyes settled on her.

"You shouldn't have come in." The druggie looked up at Gabe.

"If I didn't you would have shot her," Gabe replied, as he moved to block the man's view of Tam.

"You know what, man? Things are supposed to happen. Now you screwed everything up, and I don't know what to do, damn it."

Tamara touched Gabes' back lightly when the guy started bouncing on the balls of his feet. He looked like he was ready to kill the both of them, and gasped when he yanked out the revolver from his waistband.

"Let her go, then you have me. I'm a cop, you'll have more leverage with me."

"That's bullshit, dude!" he screamed as he pointed the gun at Gabe. "I know she's a lawyer or something!"

"Is that what this is about, her being a lawyer?"

"I don't know, man I was just told to be here at a certain time, kill the owner and take her out. You fucked it up, you fucked it up!"

Tamara was surprised by how calm Gabe was, but then again, that was his training, and then the fact that someone had taken a hit out on her.

"Listen." Gabe said, the authority in his voice unmistakable. "If you kill either one of us, you're up for life. If you leave now, I won't chase you. I'll give you a chance to get away if you leave her unharmed."

"You'll come after me, you know you will. If not, then you'll call them cop buddies of yours the minute I walk out the door."

"I won't, I'll give you a ten-minute head start before I make a call, as long as you promise not to hurt her."

"Gabe, you can't do that," Tamara whispered, gasping when he whipped around, grabbing her upper arms as he started down at her intently.

"I'll do what I have to, to get you out of here alive," he breathed. His nostrils flaring was the only sign of his emotions. "Do you understand me?"

"Yes," she whispered, watching as his pupils grew with the adrenaline running through his veins. Her gaze slowly moved when she saw the druggie jumping up and down, crying about not knowing what to do, and how this wasn't supposed to happen.

"No way. I can't do it. When they said take out Wong, I thought it was a guy, not a chick. I can't kill a chick. I don't care how much they offered."

"Just how much did they offer?" Gabe asked as he released Tam, shoving her back behind him.

"Two grand, and a cop. I'm not into knocking you guys off either, I'd be beaten to a pulp before I hit prison."

"Let us go."

"I can't do that man, I can't. You know what I look like."

Tamara's gaze followed as the guy stared pacing, he had the barrel of his gun at his temple and lifted her hand to Gabe's back again. "Who hired you to kill me?" she asked softly, noticing Gabe looking at her out of the corner of his eye.

"Don't know his name, just said that when it was done to meet him tonight."

"Where?" Gabe asked.

"It doesn't matter, man, because I'm not going to make it."

Gabe

She wanted to ask more questions but didn't think it was a good idea with the unstable emotions this guy was projecting. Her heart jumped and she held her breath when he whipped around, aiming the revolver right at Gabe. Her gut clenched, fear so strong gripping her insides at the thought of Gabe getting shot. "Please, please don't hurt him," she whispered as she stepped to Gabe's side. "He has nothing to do with any of this. He has a family, people who love him. Please don't hurt him."

"Tam, shut-up." Gabe breathed through clenched teeth.

When he tried to push her back behind him, she stayed her ground. "Please, I'm asking you not to hurt him."

"I don't want to. He's a cop, but I don't know what I'm supposed to do," the druggie wailed. "Don't go any where, do you hear me?!" he yelled as he backed out of the room.

As soon as they were alone Gabe turned on Tamara. "What the hell do you think you were doing?"

"Trying to get you out of here," Tam growled, yelping when he grabbed her, walking her backward to the wall.

"I'm not leaving with out you," he snapped. "And if you try something that stupid again, I'll spank your ass until it glows red, do you understand me?"

Lifting her hands to his chest, she shoved, and all she'd managed was a slight movement on his part. "Don't you tell me what to do, Detective. If I can get you out of here alive I will, and don't you ever think you'll be spanking anything of mine."

Gabe smiled, his brows arched as he lowered his lips to barely touch hers. "You won't be saying that when I have you handcuffed to my bed."

"Damn you, Gabe. This isn't the time. That guy, that guy…"

"I know Tam, I know."

Her entire body shuddered as he drew her into his embrace. "You have a bad sense of timing with the jokes, Mac Cloud."

"Who says it's a joke?" Backing up, he handed her the cell back. "Try to get a signal. I'll keep a look out."

Tamara took the phone, walking with it around the small room. "No good," she whispered. "Ooo wait." Grabbing a small box, she set it near the wall and smiled. "One line. That may be enough to get a text through."

"Send it to Sydney. Zack's with her."

Tamara typed quickly. *SOS in Mom & Pop's, guy with gun, being held with Gabe in back room.* "How's that?"

"Good. Send it."

Tamara lifted her hand as high as she could before hitting the send button. "Come on, work," she pleaded, her eyes following the small circle as it kept turning, and she grinned as she turned to Gabe. "It went through." She shoved the phone in her bra as his warm hands circled her waist, helping her down.

"Good, let's hope they get here before this guy comes back."

Tamara turned her head when she heard a cell go off.

"That's Zack."

"How do you know?"

"That's his ring tone. I'd say they got the message." Gabe noticed her moving behind him, her hand resting on his lower back as he faced the door.

Tamara gasped when she heard footsteps. "He's coming?" she breathed heavily.

"You stay behind me and keep your mouth shut, do you hear me?" he growled.

Tamara nodded, her eyes wide as the ringing came closer, faster, and the door swung open.

"Answer it, man, but don't tell them what's going on or else, I'll have to – you know," the guy said.

Tamara's gaze followed the cell as it was handed to Gabe.

"This is Gabe." his eyes staying on the guy in front of them.

"Hey, Syd just got this really weird text." Zack said.

"Yeah Marc, what's up?"

"You need me to roll them out?"

"Definitely. I'll see you guys tomorrow."

"Okay, man. I'm on it."

"Thanks a bunch, cuz, later." Gabe turned the phone off before handing it slowly to the guy, who snatched it up quickly.

"Everything's ok then?"

"Yep."

"Ok, ok. I'll go back, I need to think, think about what I'm going to do. You stay here and don't go anywhere."

Gabe waited until the door lock clicked on the opposite side before he turned to Tam, moving her back to the wall. "They'll be coming," he whispered. "I need you to stay as low to the ground as possible in case bullets fly."

"But I thought that was…"

"It was Zack. We use codes if one of us is in trouble. That's why he has a ring tone, and his name doesn't pop up on the screen. Now stay down, all right?" He moved her behind a few boxes; he lifted another to set on top and stopped. Meeting her gaze, he leaned down, his lips brushing hers softly. "I'm going to be behind the door so when they come, and the guy tries to get in here, he won't see either of us, and I can jump him from behind. I need you to stay down and out of sight, all right, Tam?"

Tamara nodded. "Yeah." She grabbed his arm and kissed him quickly. "Don't get hurt, okay?"

The side of Gabe's mouth lifted. "I'll try not to, counselor." Lifting the box, he made sure they hid her completely before he moved to stand behind the door and waited. Taking in deep breathes, he let them out slowly, turning his ear toward the door, and any sounds.

CHAPTER 2

GABE'S FISTS CLENCHED, BREATHING DEEPLY when he heard the unmistakable sound of two Harley's and the guy saying, "oh shit, oh shit." And then the bell above the front door chimed as the door opened. "They're here, baby. stay down." He whispered. Her whispered reply and Zack's 'hey man, how ya doing?' coming from the front. He couldn't hear everything, but knew the guy told Zack he had to leave. Zack said something in return about coke and Gabe's ears twitched with footsteps coming closer to the door.

"What the fuck, man? Where'd they go? Fuck, man. Fuck!"

"Dude, you gonna come up here so I can pay for this coke? Zack asked.

"Just leave, man, leave!"

The moment the guy stepped beyond the door, Gabe rushed him, taking him to the floor. "Zack!"

The guy screamed as Gabe pinned his arms behind his back. "Stay still you little fuck." He growled, grabbing the cuffs from Zack. "He knows a location where he's supposed to meet up with the guy who put a hit out on Tam." Rising, he yanked the guy up. "I want it." He met Zack's gaze as Jake took the junkie out, sirens in the distance. When Zack looked behind him, Gabe turned as Tamara stood up. "Are you all right?"

"Yeah. You?" Tam asked.

"Good. I want you with me on the back of the bike. We need to go to the station."

"I can drive."

"That may be, but you're not going to. Not with what just happened. You're riding with me." He met her gaze and when her lips parted he raised a brow.

"Fine, ok then. But I want a word with that guy before Jake brings him in."

Gabe turned fully toward Tamara. "For what reason?"

"What the hell do you mean for what reason? He tried to kill me, Gabe. Or are you forgetting that?"

"No, I haven't forgotten, but you're not going to beat the shit out of him either. We do this right, Tamara."

Her gaze narrowed. "You don't know me."

"Oh, I'm pretty sure I do. It's the quiet, ones who always surprise you, especially when something like this happens. We all have it in us Tam. You don't think I want to slam that piss ant's head into the wall until he spills everything he knows? Why in the hell do you think I had Jake take him out of here? you haven't had to be trained on how to handle the adrenaline and emotions from what happened. Trust me," he whispered.

Tamara lifted her hand to lay her fingers on his forearm. "Okay."

The corner of his mouth lifted as he leaned down, ready to kiss her, when footsteps ran down the hall toward them, and he backed up.

"Ms. Wong are you all right?" SWAT Commander Harrison asked.

Gabe

"Yes, Commander. Thank you."

"Holy crap, Mac Cloud. Talk about being in the right place at the right time."

Gabe shook his hand. "Definitely."

"Ms. Wong, you're to come with us back to the precinct."

"She's with me." Gabe met his gaze.

"Gabe, the DA said to bring her in."

"And she's going in with me." His tone unmistakable, he was not taking no for an answer. He knew Harrison wanted to argue. He had an order to follow, but Gabe wasn't letting Tam out of his sight. Holding his hand out, he kept, Harrison's eye as Tam lay her fingers upon his and turned, leading her out.

"Shit Gabe, how am I going to explain you brought her in on your bike? She's an open target."

"Then follow close behind, because she's not leaving my side."

"Gabe, I have a skirt on." Tam said.

Gabe turned when they were by his bike and lifted her, placing her on the back. He smiled, wiggling his brows as he took the footrests out for her. "Place your feet here."

Tam moved, inching her skirt up. "Helmet?"

"When have you ever seen me wear a helmet?" Getting on, he started it up. "Hold on." Gabe pulled out with Zack and Jake on either side, slightly behind him and SWAT behind them.

"I meant for me, Mac Cloud."

"Don't worry Wong, you're fine." He yelled back. "Just keep your eyes open."

~~*~~

Tamara's lips parted, eyes wide. "Ah, yeah, I don't think so."

"Tam, this is not a choice, this is an order." D.A. Richmond said.

"I am not going to be babysat in my own home."

"You are on protective detail until we find out and have in custody who tried to kill you."

"Jonathan, come on…"

"I am not backing down from this, Tamara. It's either Gabriel Mac Cloud or SWAT, and I'm choosing Detective Mac Cloud as he's used to working in undercover situations and he looks less like a cop than anyone on SWAT."

"Geez, tell me what you really think," Gabe muttered.

"And he has specialized training from the military. So, I suggest you get used to the idea, Tam, because he's with you until this is done."

"What about a patrol car sitting in my driveway?" Tamara asked.

"No, this is a special case. We don't know if someone from our office is in on this. Someone knew you'd be at Mom and Pop's today. The guy was waiting for you, Tam."

Tam's eyes narrowed. "Okay, so what aren't you telling me?"

"I've talked it over with Captain Kline and we both think it would be a good idea if you and Detective Mac Cloud acted as though, you're, dating."

Tam's eyes widened. "Dating?!"

"Yes."

"I would never make it known I was dating anyone, especially someone who worked for the force."

"Thanks, Tam." Gabe muttered.

"No, not like that," Tam sighed as she turned to Gabe.

"I'm a private person, especially if we just started dating. I wouldn't want you being a cop or me being the ADA to interfere with our work."

"Well, it's going to get out that something is going on between you two." Jonathan said. "After all, Gabe refused to let you ride with SWAT and almost took Harrison's head off when it came into question."

Tamara held Gabe's gaze. "I suppose you're right. But don't think you can boss me around in my home, Mac Cloud."

Gabe smiled. "You are no fun."

~~*~~

Tamara glanced into the rearview mirror as he followed her car into the three-car garage and the moment he was on the side of her car, she hit the button to close the door. Getting out of her car, she met him by his bike. "Gabe."

"Yeah?"

"Do you think this is a good idea?"

"Which part?"

Tam met his gaze. "We both know we're attracted to each other. Is it a good idea for you to be detailing me?"

"Afraid I won't do my job?"

"No, I'm afraid I'll attack and distract you."

Gabe smiled as he followed her to the door. "You may attack me, sweetheart, but you won't distract me.

Tam turned to look at him.

"At least not until this is over. Now scoot your boot and let me check it out before you go in."

Tam shook her head, the corners of her mouth lifting as she watched him take his gun out to clear her home.

Tam waited until he yelled, all clear, before entering the

kitchen. Setting her purse and keys on the small desk, she grabbed her apron out of the pantry. "What do you want for dinner? I'm starving." Smiling when he walked back in, holstering his gun. "I always start cooking when I come home, I need the normalcy right now."

"Understandable, Anything I can do to help?"

"Can you chop garlic?" she smiled, liking how he washed his hands before delving into helping her out.

"You have a cute place." Gabe said as she set a dinner plate in front of him.

"Thanks, my sister decorated it for me."

"Your sister?"

Tam chuckled. "Yeah, I have no decorating sense at all." Sitting down, she met his gaze. "Did you see my office?"

"Yeah."

"That's the only room I was allowed to touch. CJ calls me eclectic, I like mixing different styles."

"Then that's your style." He pointed his fork at her. "Why let her change you?"

Tam shrugged. "Because I'm the ADA and I should have a clean line, classic and modern home, in case I have to entertain."

"Now I know those are her words and not yours."

"Yeah, but she's right, and I like what she did. Trust me, I stopped her at several points." Smiling she took a bite.

"Are you putting me in the guest room?"

"Do you want to sleep in the guest room?"

Gabe smiled. "I think you know better than that. But Tam, don't change your routine because I'm here. Do what you do every night: work, read, play a game on your phone, walk around naked. I'm good."

Gabe

Tam chuckled as he wiggled his eyebrows. "Oh, I bet you'd love that, Mac Cloud."

~~*~~

Tam did what he said. After loading the dishwasher, she went to work on some cases in her office. She liked that he'd pop his head in to check on her. The third time he did, she put her small TV on and had him sit on her lounger with the game on. He didn't bother her. She liked working with noise in the background and usually something that would not catch her attention where she'd want to stop and watch.

Closing the file, Tamara shut her system down before turning to Gabe. "So, you were in the military?"

"Yeah."

"Which branch?"

"Army."

"Are you going to tell me or am I going to have to beat it out of you, Mac Cloud?"

Gabe grinned. "Only if you use a flogger."

Tam sighed. "Fine, but you have to use it on me after."

"Woot! Damn baby, yes!"

Tam laughed with him. "Gabe."

"Okay, okay, yes, I was a Ranger before I retired and joined the police force. You know, this really is a comfortable chair."

"I hope so, it cost me fourhundred."

"Holy crap, Tam. Are you nuts?"

Tamara chuckled. "No, like you said, it's comfortable, sometimes I'll sit in it with my laptop and work."

"Still babe, fourhundred."

Tam rose and stepped over to the chair, hiking her skit

up, she straddled him, loving his large warm hands on her hips. "You ready for bed?"

"What do you want to do in bed?"

"Anything but penetration."

Gabe frowned. "Why?"

"We can touch, kiss, feel, but no penetration. That way it gives us a chance to get to know each other and what we like."

"You're evil."

Tam chuckled. "No, I'm not." Leaning down, she took his ear lobe between her teeth.

Gabe groaned. "Challenge accepted."

CHAPTER 3

GABE ROSE OUT OF THE chair with her in his arms, his mouth sought hers as he headed to the bedroom. With one knee on the bed, he set her down. Breaking the kiss, he drew back, his gaze meeting hers, hands traveling up her thighs, pushing her skirt up, fingers sliding over silk panties. Lowering his gaze, Gabe placed soft kisses on each leg as he drew her panties down. Her thighs spread wider and he nipped the side of her knee when she arched her pelvis.

"Gabe, please."

Gabe smiled as he ran his tongue over her calf. "In time. This was your idea remember?" He didn't give her a chance to answer as he lowered his mouth to her mound, tongue flicking out to tease her clit. Her pelvis lifted, and he swiped his tongue slowly over the little nub, hands moved to her hips, holding her as he leisurely continued.

"Gabe." Her body quivered as she met his gaze.

Moving his mouth, he teased her labia to keep her from coming. Her scent and sounds were driving him crazy, his cock so damn hard he swore if he moved he'd explode. He'd been wanting this for so long, Tam spread wide and waiting for his tongue to taste her and he wasn't disappointed. Drawing back when she hit the cusp of orgasm, he nipped and sucked his way back to her mouth.

"Oh, Gabe, why did you stop?"

He smiled with her panting. His tongue tracing her bottom lip. "You wanted to get to know each other, this isn't just about sex, Tamara, or is that what you want?"

Tam groaned as he sucked on her ear lobe. "No, I, I mean, yes, I want to know you, and no, it's not about just sex."

"Good, then we play my way." He leaned back to sit on his knees. "I want you to sit up and take your clothes off." When she started unbuttoning her shirt lying down, he smacked the inside of her thigh. Her surprised "yip" and wide eyes had her gaze meeting his.

"I gave you an order. Disobey again and I will be tanning your ass. Now sit up and take your clothes off." He kept her gaze as she knelt on the bed, eyes lowering as her slim fingers started unbuttoning her silk shirt.

"Gabe?"

"Hmm."

"Are you into domination?"

"Yep." His gaze lifted to hers. "You okay with that?"

"Yes."

Her breathless reply had him smiling. "Have you ever been dominated, Tam?"

"No. I've wanted to try it, but—"

"But?"

"I've never met anyone I wanted to do it with, until now."

Gabe drew the silk shirt up, having her duck her head under it to bring the material to the front and let it puddle on her wrists. "I've waited a long time for you, Tam."

Unclasping her front-hooked bra, he palmed her breasts as they spilled out. "We'll take it slow, but I expect you to be honest with me about your comfort zone."

"You won't share me, will you?"

"Do you want me to?"

"I, well… no, not really."

Gabe smiled as he leaned down, taking her nipple into his mouth. Good, because he didn't want to share her. "I also like it rough, sweetheart. It's just who I am." His teeth closed on her nipple.

"Oh, good."

Unzipping her skirt, he moved back. "Finish undressing." When she did what he asked with no questions, his cock twitched. He knew they were attracted to each other, but for her to follow his commands turned him on even more. When she went to undo the button at her wrist, he stopped her. "Leave them." Moving off the bed, he took the shirt in the middle and drew it toward him until she followed. Lifting her arms, he placed the material on a hook slipped over the top of the door. Going behind her, he grabbed her waist, having her back up just a bit, until her arms were stretched but not uncomfortable, then used his foot to tap hers further apart. "You do not cum until I say so." Gabe drew his fingers lightly across her hip and lower back. "Red means stop. I will not stop no matter what unless you say red, do you understand?"

"Yes."

"Like I said, we'll start slow, but I want you to know what the stop word is. You won't need it tonight." Removing his clothes, he stood behind her, his dick up and aching. "Were you thinking to tease me by no penetration?"

"No, not tease." She gasped, back arched when his

shaft ran the length of her pussy. "I, I just wanted to—oh my—"

"Continue." Leaning over her back, he took ahold of her breasts.

"Like tantra, I wanted to get to know your body."

"Hmmm, I like tantra." He tweaked her nipples. "But not tonight." Placing a hand on the door for stability, he pumped harder, his cock rubbing her clit mercilessly. His hand moved from her breast to her throat, squeezing just enough. Her head came back, and hips arched into his thrusts. When her body quivered, he leapt back with a growl. His body shook from the need to orgasm. Her cry of the same drew his gaze back to her. She was going to be the death of him. Usually he had no issues controlling his orgasms. Removing the material from the hook, he took her back to the bed. He had her sit on the edge of the bed with her legs over his shoulders as he knelt and delved into her moist heat with his mouth, her gasp and movement had his hands on her hips holding her down as he sucked her clit.

"Oh God, Oh God, Gabe, please!"

"Cum for me." His tongue hit her clit and she was flying over the edge. Gabe stayed on her, slowing his movements as her orgasm subsided. Gabe stood leaning over her with a smile. "You alive?"

Her body shook, and he chuckled. "No."

Unbuttoning the pearls at her wrists and drew the shirt off, tossing it down with her skirt and panties. "Come on beautiful. Let's get you into bed." Lifting her to sit he met her gaze.

"What about you?"

"We'll take care of me tomorrow."

Gabe

Her gaze lowered. "Your cock says otherwise."

"Tam." He groaned when her fingers wrapped around his shaft.

"Let me suck your cock Gabe, I want to."

His knees almost gave out when her soft lips closed over his head and suddenly he was lying on the bed with her over him. She sucked more than half his cock into her mouth. "Damn baby." It didn't take long between her sucking and stroking his shaft for his release. "Tam, I'm going to—" his fingers gripped her hair to pull her off him, but she was fighting him. "Aahhh." He watched her gag a bit, through his pleasure-soaked mind, but she didn't back off. She kept sucking him, easing up when he finished. She sucked him gently, running her tongue around him, in a cleaning motion until he was soft and then she took his lax cock all the way in, sucking as she drew back, her tongue swirled on the top of his head.

"God, baby."

Tamara smiled as she rose up over him, placing soft kisses on his mouth.

~~*~~

Tamara glowered at Gabe. "How does me walking around the house naked have anything to do with you detailing me?"

Gabe grinned as she crossed her arms. "It will make me happy, and a happy detail is a good detail."

"You're so full of shit, Mac Cloud."

"What? It's true."

Tam stepped up to him, poking him on the chest. "I told you not to even think of bossing me around. What we do in the bedroom has nothing to do with anything else."

Gabe grabbed her finger. "It's not only the bedroom, sweetheart."

Her lips parted as he brought her finger to his mouth, sucking on it. "You know what I mean."

"I do."

Tam followed him as he lowered her hand and led her over to the couch. She sat on his lap when he positioned her between his legs. "Well, I'm not getting naked. Don't you have anything else to do on a Saturday?"

"Nope, that's tomorrow. Breakfast with the brothers."

"And who's going to detail me then?" She lifted her leg across his.

"You're going with me."

"The hell I am." Tam leaned back to meet his gaze. "I have stuff to do. I'm not following you around."

"We can do your stuff while we're out."

"Gabe, go do your boy thing, I'll be fine."

"My boy thing?" he chuckled.

"Yes, I know you guys have breakfast every Sunday, no girls."

"And how do you know that?"

"Sydney. She's mentioned it a few times when we talk at work."

"Ah, the best sister-in-law I've ever had."

Tam frowned. "Don't you have another one? I thought your oldest brother got married while Zack was detailing Sydney."

"Yep, true enough."

"I'm not understanding."

Gabe sighed. "We don't get along too well."

Tam sensed he didn't want to talk about it, maybe because they were just getting to know each other. Leaning down, she kissed him softly. "I'll be okay tomorrow Gabe. I stay home on Sundays in my pj's, hair in a ponytail and clean house, while I do laundry."

"Will you walk around naked for me tomorrow?"

Tam chuckled. "As long as you're alone when you come home."

Gabe attacked her mouth, moving her to lay under him on the couch, when the doorbell rang.

Tam's eyes were wide as she met his gaze. "I have no one coming today."

Gabe withdrew his revolver as he approached the door when there was a knock.

"Gabe, it's Jake."

"For Christ's sake." Holstering his piece, he checked through the peep hole before opening the door. "What the hell, little brother?"

"Kline sent me," he stated as he entered. "Ms. Wong."

"Detective." Tam replied as she rose from the couch.

"Captain Kline sent me to ask you about a file you had on your computer at the office. The one with all the threats you've received."

"Threats?" Gabe said, turning to meet her gaze.

"I'm not only a lawyer, Gabe, I'm an assistant district attorney. My mentor taught me to keep everything, no matter how small."

"Right," Jake said. "There was this one. We didn't think anything of it at first, but being a jilted lover and another attorney…"

"Wait one minute." Tam said, her hand up to stop him. "Are you referring to Jenkins?"

"Yes ma'am."

"Then let's get something straight right now. Ralph Jenkins was never a lover of any kind, much to his dissatisfaction, and if you had bothered to read those emails, you would have seen that for yourself, Detective."

"I apologize, Ms. Wong."

"What the hell, Jake," Gabe said. "How'd you let that slip by you?"

"Sorry, I'm sorry, I should have checked the material myself."

"Tam, give us a minute, would you."

Tam's brows lifted. "Sure, as long as you don't beat him to a pulp." She turned when he glared at her from the corner of his eye. "You have until I get three cups of coffee poured, and no yelling. I do have neighbors, Mac Cloud." Striding into the kitchen, she listened as he read Jake the riot act. "Coffee's poured. Hurry up, Detective's. I need to get my Saturday shopping done."

~~*~~

Tamara smiled when Gabe picked up a toy and squeezed it. "I think that's a good one, Gabe."

"Won't it make an awful lot of noise?" he asked, squeezing it again.

"That's the point." Grinning she took it from him and set it in the basket. "I'm auntie, I get noise makers to get back at my sister for all the shit she did to me when we were kids."

"That's just wrong."

"Trust me, when Zack and Sydney's baby is old enough to play with toys, you'll do it."

"But won't they do it back when you have kids? I mean, if you want kids."

Tam met his gaze and smiled. "Of course, I want kids. Not six like my sister, but yes, I'd like a couple."

"Six, damn. I don't blame you there. Mom has four of us, all boys and I don't know how she pulled that off."

"Were you trouble-makers, Gabe?"

"Hell yeah." He chuckled. "We're all pretty close together. So, when we did it, we did it big."

"I know what you mean. My sister Charlotte, she's the one with the six. She was older than me by seven years, so she really didn't want anything to do with me or our little sister Jenny. But Jenny and I." She chuckled. "Oh, holy crap, did my mom have her hands full with us."

"Was your mom or dad the punisher?"

"Oh, defiantly my mom. She's a good ole country girl from Kentucky and didn't put up with any of it."

"So, you're daddy's girl." He grinned.

Tam met his gaze as they stepped in line at the cash register. "Yes. I talk to him every Sunday."

"And your mom?"

"Mom passed about three years ago."

"I'm sorry."

Tam smiled up at him as he rubbed her back. "Me too, it's been hard. That's one of the reasons I took the job here. I needed to get away from everything so familiar."

"Understandable. I'm sorry for your loss, but I'm glad you took the job here."

"Me too." She whispered as her phone rang. "Wong."

"You're dead."

Tam held the phone away, thrusting it at Gabe. "They said I was dead."

CHAPTER 4

GABE GRABBED THE PHONE. "WHO is this?"

"I know you're not dating her, Detective, the little whore she's shown herself to be. Stay too close and you might get hit too."

"Son of a bitch." Gabe growled as the perp hung up. Closing her phone, he paid for the toys and took Tam to the side. Keeping her away from the glass windows, he called Zack. "Tam was just threatened on her cell. A guy called and said he knew we weren't dating."

"Where are you?" Zack asked.

"Toy store down at the mall."

"I'm on my way."

"Do not put this on open channel, I don't trust anyone but family now."

"Right there with you brother. Stay safe, we're rolling out."

Gabe hung up and stuck his cell back in his pocket.

"Gabe."

Gabe turned at her whisper, her eyes were wide, arms wrapped around her waist. "Aw, babe." Bringing her into his embrace, he held her close. She was scared, and he didn't blame her; not only was this guy stalking her and tried to kill her, he knew her contact information.

"Sir, do you need me to call 9-1-1?"

Gabe

Gabe turned his head to see the cashier standing next to them.

"I overheard some of what she said, and I think you need the cops."

"I am the cops." Flipping his wallet open, he displayed his badge. "Thanks for the concern. I have back up on the way."

"Oh, ok. Ah, ma'am. Would you like a bottle of water? You look like you might pass out."

"Thank you, but I'm fine," Tam said.

Gabe saw the small smile she gave the girl and tightened his hold on her. "If he has your phone number, I'm not liking the idea of going back to your house, Tam."

"Gabe, I just thought of something. What if it's not a guy? I mean, the voice was a voice- synthesized male, but what if that was done on purpose?"

Gabe met her gaze as the roar of Harley's approached.

~~*~~

Tam turned to glare at Gabe. "When you said a safe house, this was the last thing I thought of."

"It's the safest place I know of." He set her bag on the sofa. "The entire bar is filled with undercover cops; my uncle is the bartender and we have a camera and security system like you haven't seen. So yes. We're staying."

"Gabe, I can't stay here."

"Give me one good reason why."

Tam met his gaze. "Well, you're a little loud."

"Loud. Loud at what?"

"Sex, well oral sex and I know I'm not quiet either, and I will not have a bar full of cops…"

Gabe busted out laughing.

Tam smacked his arm. "Don't you laugh at me."

"Baby, with all the noise and music going on down there, they wouldn't here an orgy going on up here. Besides, the bedroom is a bit more, soundproof. Zack made sure of that when he rehabbed the living area."

"So, they won't be able to hear us?"

"Nope."

"Oh, well, okay then." She smiled, lifting her travel bag, she carried it to the bedroom. She didn't have her cell on her as Gabe gave it to his brothers to have checked out. He wouldn't even let her bring her laptop. "Hey, Gabe."

"Yeah?" he answered right behind her, tossing his bag on the bed.

"What kind of chaise is that? It's a bit different than the ones I've seen."

"It's a tantric chair."

Tam whipped around to meet his gaze. "Tantric?"

"Uh-huh. You said you wanted to try it, right?"

"Well, yes, but- well- where did it come from?"

"The other room. I had to dust it off, forgot I even had it until you mentioned it last night."

"Oh." Her gaze went to the light tan leather lounger.

"Mmmmm, your nipples are hard."

"I know." She breathed, chest rising with a deep breath. "Maybe- maybe we should eat first."

They both turned with a knock at the front door. Tam followed Gabe out as he answered it see their Uncle Walt standing there. "Oh Walt." She said as he turned. "Don't do what you did to Sydney and Zack to us. You know, barging in every time they got hot and heavy. I'm not a target and we won't answer the door. So if you come in anyway, you may see us having sex and we won't stop." Smiling she met

Gabe

his gaze head on, Gabe chuckled, and Walt nodded with a smile as he headed downstairs. Tam turned for the galley style kitchen as Gabe shut and locked the door.

Dinner done, dishes washed, she turned to Gabe, took him by the hand and led him to the bedroom.

"What are you trying to tell me, Ms. Wong?"

"It's Ms. Wong, when you have me bent over my desk." Tam replied as she shut the door and turned to him. His brow lifted as their gazes met, drawing her t-shirt over her head, Tam tossed it to the floor, and stepped up to him. Drawing his t-shirt out of the waistband of his jeans, she lifted it over his muscled chest, and he helped her take it the rest of the way off. When she had them both naked, she led him over to the lounger. She looked at it for a moment before having him straddle it and lean against the back before she did the same, facing him. Tam was surprised he let her lead, but he did, and she kinda liked it. Moving her legs over his she moved closer to him, his hard dick inches from her as they sat looking at each other. Lifting her hand, she cupped the side of his face, Following her thumb with her gaze, she moved it slowly over his warm skin, his five o'clock shadow tickling her fingertip. Tam caressed her thumb over his bottom lip, a gasp escaping her when he nibbled on it. Leaning in, she replaced her thumb with her lips. Her hands cupped either side of his face as she slowly tasted him, her mouth slowly moving to his ear, then his neck.

Tam could feel his heartbeat quicken as she loved his neck. Her hands moved to his chest; his breathing had picked up, as did hers and to know she affected him like he did her was exciting. His chest was hard and muscled as though he went to the gym daily. His pecs moved under her ministrations and she leaned forward, placing a kiss above his nipple. Tam froze when someone knocked at the bedroom door.

"What the fuck?" Gabe snarled. "What?!"

"It's Zack. We need to talk."

Tam lifted her gaze to meet Gabe's.

"I'm sorry, babe. He wouldn't bother us unless it was important."

"I know." Tam leaned into his hand when he cupped the side of her face. His fingers slid into her hair as he brought her closer for a kiss.

"Gabe!" Zack belted out.

"In a fucking minute!"

Tam sighed as she drew back and rose off the lounge chair. Grabbing the robe she'd brought with her, she handed him a pair of shorts.

"Thanks."

"Don't knock his block off."

"I won't. It just pisses me off."

"Oh, tell me about it."

Gabe turned her to him. "No babe, it was your time to explore, to…"

Tamara kissed him silent. Wrapping her arms around his waist, her palms lay on his back. "I'll get my chance, now let's go see what he's so fired up about."

"You're beautiful, you know that?"

"Hmmm," she smiled.

"Gabriel!" Zack yelled.

"Good God! We're coming already!"

~~*~~

Gabe

Tam stared at Zack. "Are you sure?"

"Unfortunately, yes." Zack answered. "It's a good thing Gabe had you leave all electronics at the house or with us. Listen, Tamara. The D.A. doesn't want you in the office on Monday. He's going to have the entire building checked and until he does, and we have a team set up there, you're on house detail."

Tam sighed. "And what am I supposed to do with no phone, no laptop, no work? Sitting around all day is not something I'm used to."

"I'm sure Gabe can find something to fill your day."

Tam glowered. "Not funny, Detective."

"All right, all right. Anyway, we have a few more things to go through. Have you ever brought your laptop to the office?"

Tam shook her head. "No," her gaze lowering as she remembered. "But I brought the office home."

"What do you mean?" Gabe asked.

"I had a small office party at my house. It was before Zack started detailing Sydney."

"Do you remember who came?"

"Ah, Sydney, but I trust her impeccably."

Zack chuckled. "That's good."

"Um, Jonathan and his wife, Caitlin, Susie and her husband, and Sheri and her girlfriend." Tam sat there. She heard Zack and Gabe talking but didn't pay attention. There was something there, just at the back of her memory. She'd thought it odd, but... "Caitlin!" Her gaze met Gabe's. "I thought it was weird but dismissed it. I caught Caitlin in my office, sitting at my desk. My laptop was open. I always close it when I'm finished. She told me she needed to grab medicine or something out of

32

her coat, but she was nowhere near the coats. They were sitting on the recliner."

"That could be it." Zack said.

"But I have a password on my laptop. She couldn't have gotten in."

"Are you so sure she didn't know what it was?"

"At this point, I'm not too sure about anything." The warm heat of Gabe's hand on her back, calmed her. "But why would Caitlin do something like this?"

"How well do you know her?" Gabe asked.

"Not well, I mean, she's Jonathan's secretary. I really don't see her at all unless I go down for a meeting. Sydney has more contact with her than I do."

"Has she ever shown any signs of aggression toward you?"

"No, she's always smiling and pleasant."

"Is she ever in the office before you arrive?" Zack asked.

"Ah, yes. I've waved to her as I walked by Jonathan's office."

"Did you get anything on the call earlier?" Gabe asked.

"No, if it is Caitlin, she's using a burner phone. We can't trace it," Zack said.

"And a voice synthesizer, has Jake come up with anything?"

"No, but he's still looking."

"Are you going to pull her in for questioning?" Tamara asked.

"We don't have enough yet, but now that I know she was in your home and your office, I can start looking at another angle. I'll have Jake and Tech start searching a couple different areas."

Gabe

"You're being awful careful not to tell me what or where you're going to be looking."

Zack shrugged. "It's not personal, Tamara. It's still an ongoing investigation."

"I know, I know. Well, if you're done with me, I'm going to bed." Patting Gabe's arm as she turned, Tam headed for the bedroom and shut the door behind her. Caitlin, why in the hell would Caitlin want her dead? She barely said two words to her on any given day. Sighing, Tam removed the robe, laying it on the foot of the bed before delving under the covers. She could hear Gabe and Zack speaking in low tones, and the beat of music coming up from below lulled her to sleep.

~~*~~

"Don't give me that, I'm fine here. Go," Tam snapped as she turned and met Gabe's gaze.

"I'm not leaving your side until this is over."

"That's bullshit, Gabe and you know it. I'm safe here and Walt is right downstairs." Tamara wrapped her arms around his waist, her head laying on his chest. She loved how tall he was, at least a foot taller than her five foot four. When his arms wrapped around her, she snuggled into him. "Gabe, I'll be fine. Go have breakfast with your brothers."

"I'd rather stay here and let you explore."

Tam chuckled. "We have all night and tomorrow for exploration." Looking up, she met his gaze as she grabbed his bottom lip between her teeth. "Seeing as how I'm banned from the office and everything."

"Really?" his brow lifted.

"Mmmm, why don't we plan on playing some pool downstairs after we eat, have a couple of drinks, then I'll walk around naked for you."

"Why don't we go straight to naked?"

"Well, we do have all day tomorrow."

Tam was glad for the time alone. Sighing, she crashed on the sofa. While she enjoyed being with Gabe, she didn't have a lot of time for herself or to think about what was happening. Someone, maybe Caitlin, was out to kill her. Never had she thought someone would try to kill her, especially someone she may have let into her home. She knew Gabe would be discussing the case with his brothers and he wouldn't relay much to her, either because it was an on-going case, or he wanted to protect her, but she'd find out eventually. She didn't really feel like going down to play pool or having a couple of drinks, but wanted something else to do to take her mind off everything. Rising, she went to the bedroom.

"Tam." Gabe called out. "Sorry it took so long, I had to go to the station. Where are you?"

"In here. Did you eat lunch and dinner?"

"Yeah, you?"

"Yes, are you alone?"

"Yeah."

Tam smiled as she stepped into the door way, his shirt just hitting her thighs. "I was thinking to hell with drinks and pool."

"Damn, baby."

Tam walked up to him, swaying her hips, her high heels click-clacked as she kept his gaze. Drawing her finger down from his pecs to his waistband, her hand moved with his indrawn breath. "Gabe."

"Hmm?"

Gabe

"I want to play."

"Good."

Tingles ran through her as his fingers gripped the back of her head, tugging on her hair. Tamara leaned into him, their mouths met hungrily, and her nipples ached as they rubbed against his chest. Her lips parted on a gasp when his hand reached around and squeezed her ass, drawing her closer to him.

"Suck my cock."

"Yes, sir." She breathed, a slight smile at the corners when she nipped his neck, loving his growl. Her fingers found his button and zipper, lowering it slowly, her lips trailing down. His groan had her pussy clenching the moment her lips touched his engorged head.

"Fuck, sweetheart, I love your mouth."

Tamara moaned as she went down on him, sucking and twirling her tongue over shaft and head, his pre-cum tingling her taste buds. Tam looked up as the door started to open, her mouth never leaving Gabe as he leaned back with his weight shutting it and whoever was trying to come through out.

"Finish for me, sweet."

His low guttural tone let her know he was close, lifting her hand, she grabbed his shaft, stroking it hard as she sucked.

"Tam, I'm going to – "

Tamara grabbed his ass, bringing his cock deeper into her mouth and then his hips bucked under her, taking his salty essence, she waited until he was finished before swallowing. Glancing up, his head rested against the door, his chest rising with his heavy breathing. Sucking him gently, he twitched as she withdrew her mouth.

"Go to the bedroom, baby."

"Gabe…"

"Go to the bedroom, Tam. Someone's about to get their ass beat."

Tamara let him help her up and glanced back as she headed to the bedroom. "Should I get dressed?"

"Not if I can help it."

Tam met his gaze as she shut the bedroom door. He was stuffing his cock back into his jeans. Damn it, every time they got started here, someone was at the friggin' door. If this kept up, she was going to insist they go back to her house.

"Tam, you may want to come out here." Gabe said.

"God, are you serious?"

"I wouldn't ask if I wasn't."

Tam grabbed a pair of shorts out of her bag and swung the door open. She didn't give shit her hair was down and messed up and saw Zack, Jake, and Marc, their cousin there. "What?"

Gabe's brows went up with a smile as Zack started apologizing.

"Yeah, yeah, Mac Cloud. Stuff the apologies, and get to why in the hell you're bothering us again."

"Sorry, Tamara," Zack said. "Jake and I took Caitlin down for questioning and I hate to say it, but I don't think it's her."

"Explain."

"For one, she has alibis, not just one or two people, around six. She was at a party yesterday and her cell wasn't in her possession."

"I thought you guys said burner phone?"

"We did and we're still thinking so. But she had no other phone available to her. They locked all cells and keys up in a lock box and everyone was still there when we arrived this morning."

"So how do you know she didn't sneak out?"

Zack glanced over at Gabe.

"She's a big girl, give it to her straight." Gabe said as he leaned on the kitchen counter.

"It was a sex party," Zack started. "When we arrived this morning about six, she was in between two women, who confirmed she hadn't left since she arrived. They ah, they didn't stop playing until about four this morning."

"Ok, so what's the rest?"

"Caitlin admitted to having a crush on you, said it really pissed her ex-girlfriend off. To the extent of the ex making threats against you."

"Wonderful." Tam leaned against Gabe, just enough to feel the heat of his body. It was soothing. "So, I can go to work tomorrow?"

"No, the D. A. still wants to clear the building."

Tamara met Gabe's gaze when he wrapped his other arm around her, to sit on her hip. "Is that it?"

"Not quite." Jake said. "The D. A. also wants you detailed while working. It's either one of us or…"

"Oh, hell no." Tam straightened up.

"Tam, listen to what he has to say." Gabe said.

"I'm in a secure building, even more secure tomorrow after they finish whatever they're doing. I don't need a babysitter."

"Maybe not," Zack said. "But I want an officer there."

Tamara met Zack's gaze. "Sydney." Lowering her gaze, she understood why Zack wanted an officer there with what was happening. Sydney was pregnant with their child and she couldn't blame him. "All right, but damn it, if you put John, her cousin in my office I'll rip your heads off. They get along like oil and water since she was targeted and I'm not having that shit with this shit going on." Tam lifted her gaze back to Zack's. He looked relieved that she hadn't said no. Hell, he might have pulled Sydney out altogether, leaving her with some temp who didn't know what the hell they were doing.

"What about the new officer," Jake said. "Ah, she just transferred in from the Midwest, I think."

"No, it was Florida," Marc said. "Andres, Catia Andres."

"Right, and no one knows her really, not at the D. A.'s office. She hasn't had a chance to come up on any cases. But from what I hear, she's good."

"We can put her in plain clothes." Zack said. "Make it look like Syd's training her to help out when she goes out on maternity leave."

"Yeah, ok," Tamara replied. "That would work."

"All right, I'll run it by the D. A. and Kline."

"Oh, Zack," Tam said as they turned to the door. "I want the damn key."

"What?"

"The key. While I'm staying here, I'll be damned if one of you walk in on us again." Holding her hand out, her brow arched as Zack stood there looking at her, while Gabe chuckled.

"Now."

CHAPTER 5

TAMARA TURNED, KEY IN HAND and door locked. Her gaze on Gabe. "So, Detective, I believe we left off somewhere."

Gabe grinned. "We sure as hell did."

Tam chuckled as she headed toward the bedroom.

"Have anything on under those shorts?"

"Nope." Tam turned as he shut and locked the door. "Extra precaution?"

"Oh, hell yeah. Why don't you strip and get on the bed."

"I thought I'd have a chance to explore."

"You will…"

"No, Detective, I want my time to explore." Tamara smiled when he cocked a brow. "Why don't we undress and get on the bed."

"I think I've been lenient with you."

"A little, but every time we start getting to know each other, except for the first night we've been together, we always get interrupted. Besides, it's nice being on the receiving end." Kicking her shorts off Tam lifted her gaze to see he was already naked. "Sit on the bed for me."

"Tam, I've been on the receiving end. You were sucking my cock before they tried to come in."

Tam followed him and had him sit with his back on the

pillows before straddling him. "Yeah, but to lie here and be petted and caressed, it feels nice, Gabe. I want you to relax and enjoy."

"I won't be able to totally relax until this is over. You're the one I'm worried about."

Tam ran her fingers down his shoulder to his elbow, slowly. "I know. Just let me do this, okay?" Meeting his gaze, she leaned in for a soft kiss. She couldn't remember the last time she took her time kissing a man. She ran her tongue along his lower lip before nibbling it. Her lips soft as she kissed the soreness she caused. Tamara lifted her hands to either side of his face, her thumb caressed his cheekbone. Her fingers moved to the back of his head, into his short hair and tugged gently. His chest rose, breathing heavy, a moan escaped his parted lips when she ran the tip of her tongue over his lower lip again. Sweeping it slowly along, she delved inside and increased pressure when Gabe kissed her back. "You have the softest lips."

"Chapstick."

Tam smiled as she slid the tip of her tongue inside his mouth with soft darting motions; when he tried to become aggressive, she slowed the kiss back down. He was a natural dominator, he liked to be in control, and she liked him in control of her. So far, she'd received nothing but pleasure at his hands. But tonight, he was hers to control, and she had a feeling he'd let her be in control when she wanted, because he seemed to like it too. Rubbing her nose against his, she kissed him softly, her hands running down his arms, bringing his hands to her hips and up to her breasts. "I love my nipples played with." Lowering her mouth, she took one of his nipples into his mouth and nipped when he tweaked hers. They both groaned. Her hand reached down to his shaft.

"God, Tam."

Her nose nudged his again, hot breath teasing his ear. "I love your cock, Gabe." Bringing his lobe into her mouth, she sucked and nipped. His moan let her know her words and touches turned him on. "I can't wait until it's in me. My pussy clenches every time I think of sucking you into my mouth."

"Fucking A, baby."

Tam screeched, eyes wide when she was lifted off him and laid on the bed.

"Keep that shit up and you won't be able to walk in the morning." Lifting her legs over his shoulders his mouth lowered to her mound.

Tamara groaned, her fingers clenching the bed sheet as his tongue worked her swollen clit. She didn't last long and when he lifted his fingers to tweak her nipples, her back arched as her abdomen muscles clenched, sending her over the edge with Gabe's name on her lips.

~~*~~

Tamara frowned as Gabe told Officer Andres not to let her out of her sight. "What do you think she's going to do, follow me to the bathroom?"

"Yes." Gabe said.

"Don't worry, Detective. We'll be fine." Officer Andres said.

"You have my number, right?"

"Right here."

Tam pursed her lips as Gabe turned and met her gaze. "I'm a big girl, you know."

Gabe leaned in and kissed her temple. "I know."

"Don't you placate me, Mac Cloud."

"I'm not Wong."

Tamara chuckled as Gabe hugged her to him. "I'll be fine, Gabe."

"I know you will."

"Good. Go to work and I'll see you at five."

Gabe saluted her. "Yes, Ma'am."

Tam swatted him as he headed out. Going to her desk, she started going through the mail, same thing she did every morning. It was weird walking in and not seeing Caitlin at her desk. Gabe said they had her on paid administrative leave until this was over. She could hear Sydney speaking to officer Andres as she lifted a manila envelope with her name on it. Sliding her finger under the closed seam, she peaked inside to see photos. "Oh my God." Her mouth gaped as she stared with wide eyes. "Gabe! Get me Gabe!" She hugged the photo to her chest and ran for the door as Sydney and Catia ran in. "Gabe, get Gabe."

"Okay, okay. Settle down, Tam." Sydney said. "What happened, what's that?"

"Just get me Gabe." Tam paced her office, listening to Catia on the phone with Gabe, her breathing shallow and rapid.

"Tam, sit down. My God you're going to pass out."

"What the heck is going on? I wasn't even out of the elevator." Gabe said as he walked in.

Tam ran up, grabbed him by the arm and dragged him into her office, shutting the door. "My God, Gabe. I- I was going through my mail and opened the envelope and, and—" she held out the photo. "Oh my God, how did they get in my house, how did they do this?"

Gabe

Tam wrapped her arms around her waist as he looked at the photo of them together the very first night he stayed at her house. The words 'and the whore you are' written at the bottom of the photo, of Tam laying on the bed and him going down on her.

His lips were tight as he walked over to the envelope she'd dropped onto her desk.

"How did they get it in here?"

"I don't know, honey."

"I thought- I thought they cleared the building," she said, as he set the photo upside down on top of the envelope. "Gabe?" Tam met his gaze when he turned to her, taking her in his arms. Tam hugged him as he lifted his cell, calling Zack.

"He's on his way with a crime scene tech."

"Gabe, don't let anyone see those." Tam met his gaze. "Can't they just use the envelope?"

"The writing is on the photo, let me talk to Larry, we may be able to cover the photo up."

"Gabe, they were in my house."

"I know, honey."

Tam didn't know how long he held her before a knock on the door, but she saw the outer office had more people including the D. A. who came in with Zack.

"Maybe you should stay in Gabe's safe house until this is over." Jonathan said.

"I can't miss work like that, Jonathan."

"This building is not safe for you. That was just proven."

"I have cases…"

"You are at the safe house until further notice."

Tam's gaze narrowed at his stern tone as she stared

down her boss. Unfortunately, it didn't work on him. "Fine, but I'm not happy about this."

"Jake, take her home." Gabe said.

"Wait, what?"

"I need to get some work done. Wait for Larry."

Tam nodded as he met her gaze. "Oh, right. Ok."

"Go on. You'll be fine besides Jake knows if anything happens to you, I'll string him up."

Tam smiled. "I'm sure I'll be fine." Lifting on her toes, she met his quick kiss.

"Go. I'll be there when I'm finished."

~~*~~

Tam had waited up for him most of the night. Covering her mouth with a yawn, she glanced over at Jake. "Hey, think you can take me to the gym?"

"Nope."

"Are you shitting me?"

"No, Gabe said no public areas."

"And you do everything he says?"

"Hell ya, I like my balls right where they are."

Tam chuckled. "Ok, ok – hey what about the gym at the station, It's secure?" Her gaze followed when he took his cell phone out. "Are you kidding?"

"Nope."

Tam paced until the text was answered. "Well?"

"He says that's all right, if you want to go get your stuff…"

"Yep!" Tam scooted into the bedroom, grabbing her gym bag she brought with her from the office and ran out to the living room. "All right Jakey boy, let's go."

"Really, Jakey boy?"

Gabe

Tam chuckled as he followed her out.

Tam's chest rose as she breathed deeply, she'd run on the tread mill for an hour, then hit some of the machines to tone her upper body. Now she was punching the heck out of the bag. Glancing over, she noticed officer Andres speaking with Jake before Gabe came in. She wasn't ready to stop yet. This friggin' situation pissed her off. She couldn't go home, she couldn't go to work, she couldn't even go to her own f'ing gym. And all because some damn psycho with a stalking habit chose her to target. "Fucking A!" Slamming the bag hard, she took a step back, nostrils flaring, chest rising rapidly.

"Go shower it off." Gabe called out.

Tam flung him the middle finger. "Piss off, Mac Cloud." Shaking her hands, she heard Jake's hoot of laughter as she started pacing from one end of the gym to the other. She didn't want to be near anyone right now. She just wanted to be left alone, and she wanted to beat the living crap out of the person turning her world upside down.

Goosebumps rose on her skin as her body cooled. Tam stopped pacing, her focus on the floor, as she grabbed her bag and headed to the shower.

"You ok?"

"Yeah." Tam rinsed her hair as she turned to meet Gabe's gaze. "Frustrated, pissed off, you know. So, did you find anything out?"

"Yep."

Tam turned off the water. "Well, are you going to elaborate?" Her gaze narrowed as his followed her movements of drying off. "Gabe."

"The tech's working on the writing, I talked Larry into keeping the photo covered unless absolutely necessary. Zack and I worked a lead last night, that's why I wasn't there this morning. The cameras in your house have been located and they're trying to follow the signal back to where it's transmitting to."

"Any luck with the lead?"

"I sent Jake and Andres to relieve Mitch and Marc."

Tam nodded as she dressed. So, he really wasn't taking any chances, keeping the detail in the family or friends they trusted. "I think they like each other."

"Mitch and Marc?"

Tam chuckled. "No, Jake and Catia." Tossing the towel in the bin, she grabbed her bag.

Gabe shrugged. "Not my concern. Hungry?"

"Yes, thank you."

Tam stayed next to Gabe as they stepped out of the station. Going down the stairs, Tam looked to the left past Gabe when tires screeched. The air caught in her lungs as Gabe flung her to the ground, the sharp sound of a gun fire close. Her nostrils flared with the smell of gun powder as Gabe opened fire on the vehicle. Her chest rose as she tried to breath, coughing with the weight of Gabe's body on top of her. Sounds exploded around her as Tam's lids fluttered, feet ran by, cars and sirens took off and Gabe turned to meet her gaze.

"Are you all right?"

"Yeah, except you're heavy." Her eyes closed as she breathed deeply when he rolled off enough for her to get a good lung full of air. Her hand reached up, rubbing his arm as he spoke with someone. His muscles twitched, and she found an odd spot, warm, wet. Glancing up, her eyes widened. "Gabe, Gabe, you've been shot." Her fingers covered with his blood.

"The medics are coming, just stay still for me."

"But you've been shot. My God Gabe, get off me so I can help you."

"Tamara!"

Her wide gaze whipped up to his.

"I can't."

"What? Why? Were you shot somewhere else?"

"No honey, you were."

"Wh-haat?"

"You were hit in your thigh, I'm applying pressure and I need you to stay still."

"But what about you?"

Gabe grinned. "I've had worse. Now stay still, the ambulance is here."

Tam did as he said and stayed still as the EMT's tended to both of them. Her gaze never wavered from his location until they lifted her on a gurney. "Gabe."

"I'm right here. I'm going with you."

Tam took his hand. "Are you all right?"

"Grazed."

Tam saw the exchanged look between the EMT and Gabe. "You're such a damn liar, Mac Cloud."

"Yeah, yeah. Be good Wong. They need to get you loaded."

Tam kept an eye on him as they loaded her and worked on her some more. Gabe was talking to his Captain before he turned and met her gaze.

"Ma'am, do you have high blood pressure?" an EMT asked.

"No, no medical conditions, I'm allergic to codeine and I don't do pain meds."

"You can discuss that with the doctors. Gabe, we're ready to roll."

Tam met Gabe's gaze as he entered the back and sat next to her. Reaching over, she twined her fingers with his as they hung between his legs. "It's starting to hurt now."

"That's because the adrenaline is leaving, and they have pressure on the wound."

Her sight blurred with the tears gathering, lowering her eyes as she wasn't one to cry in font of anyone or in public, but damn.

"Hey, are you all right?"

She squeezed his fingers. "Yeah, it's just a lot to process and I wasn't in the best of moods when it happened." When he leaned over, she met his gaze as he ran his lips lightly across hers.

"It's going to be ok, honey."

"Damn it, Mac Cloud." Lifting her hand, she cupped the side of his face as tears flowed down her cheeks.

"Awww, sweetie." He whispered, his forehead touching Tam's.

Tam cleared her throat; her fingers skimmed his cheek and beard. "I'm all right." She smiled softly as Gabe turned his head, kissing the inside of her palm before they arrived at the hospital, then they were separated.

CHAPTER 6

GABE TURNED HIS GAZE MEETING Zack's. "Did they get the bastard?"

"No. The black and whites were able to grab the car; it's on the way to forensics. It's only a matter of time before we catch whoever it is."

Gabe sighed. "Have you heard how Tamara's doing?"

"She's still in surgery. They had to remove the bullet, and don't worry, I have John and Marc sitting outside the doors. How did your removal go?"

"Fine, I'm ready to get the hell out of here."

"Yeah about that, Kline said when they release you, you're on bed rest, house duty, what ever the hell you want to call it with Tamara until this ass is caught."

"Bullshit!"

"Gabe. I have to agree with the Captain."

"What?"

"You are wounded, and you need to take care of Tam when she's released. Besides, I think you're getting a little too close to this case."

Gabe snorted. "Like you didn't with Syd."

"Right, so stay home with Tamara at the safe house and take your time getting to know each other."

"You want me to play house?"

"Hey, it could be worse." Zack patted the end of the bed. "I'll keep you updated if anything comes up. I had them put you two in the same room."

"Smart thinking. Now, get the hell out of here and catch that bastard." Gabe frowned as he kept an eye on Zack's retreating back lifting them when a nurse walked in. "When am I being transferred to the room with Tamara Wong?"

"Right now, Detective and so you know, she's in post op. The surgery went fine, no problems. As soon as she's able, they'll get her in there with you."

"Thank you."

Gabe stood by as they transferred Tam to the bed. She was still out. "Was it a clean shot? Any nerve damage?"

"You'll have to speak with the doctor, but she did well. She'll be in and out due to the anesthesia."

Gabe nodded and the moment they left, he kicked the breaks up on his bed, moved the table aside and scooted it right up against Tam's. Setting the breaks, he hopped on, moved as close as he could, careful of the IV's and lines and closed his eyes. Fingers entwined, he let the slow rise and fall of her chest lull him to sleep.

Gabe moaned. Eyes barely open, darkness greeted him, a light from the parking lot, had him blinking. What the hell had woken him up? His gaze on the hospital's roof outside the window, he blinked several times, yawned and managed to open both eyes to the sound of Jake arguing softly with someone. Glancing at his watch, five past two in the morning.

"I am telling you, we will be moving these beds." A female voice stated.

Gabe

"Ma'am, I wouldn't try it." Jake responded.

Gabe frowned as they came closer and stood at the end of the beds. "Shut the fuck up or get the hell out."

"Detective Mac Cloud, I'm Nurse Plinkley, the floor nurse tonight and we cannot have these two beds pushed together like this, I'm sorry, but you're going to have to move."

Gabe rolled from his side onto his back enough to meet her gaze. "No, I'm sorry Nurse Plinkley. My ass isn't moving anywhere. In case you haven't noticed, we've both been shot. This is the ADA and not only my detail, but my girlfriend, so if you can find a cop who has the balls to move me from her side, then you go ahead and bring him in."

"Sir, this is not acceptable. I'm going to call security."

"It's Detective, and you go right ahead and call the rent-a-cop. Jake, hand me my cell so I can call Sheridan." Gabe's brow lifted. "You know, Tristian Sheridan, the top investor of this hospital and President of the board. That Tristian Sheridan."

"Well, that's just—"

"Yeah, went to school with him, played football and pushed each other through army basic training, so yeah, you go ahead and call security. If we're done seeing who has the biggest balls, you can leave, stay out of my sight and let us rest."

Gabe kept his gaze on her as she turned and stormed from the room. "Any new news?"

"Sleep, we'll talk in the morning." Jake grinned as he shut the door behind him.

Gabe groaned, his arm stiff, sore from the wound and rolled back over to lay his head down next to Tam.

"You are so my hero." Tamara whispered.

"That's me, my baby's hero." Leaning in, he kissed her cheek softly as she turned and nuzzled her face to his, before her breathing became even again. Gabe smiled as he cuddled back up to her side.

~~*~~

"Tell me where we stand." Gabe said as he sat on the edge of the bed.

"They were able to pull prints from the car. We're running them through the system to see if we can get a match. The bullets taken from you and Tamara are going through ballistics and the owner of the car is in holding waiting for us to talk to."

"Who is it?"

"Lydia Gulfries. She moved to the area six months ago. From what Spicer said, she had no idea how her car ended up in a drive by."

Gabe's gaze narrowed. "But you do."

"I have a theory."

"Spit it out, little brother."

"Zack will be here in ten to talk to the both of you." Jake said, as Tam rolled toward him with eyes open.

"Damn it Jake."

"Hey man, I'm just following orders."

Gabe sighed as Jake let the room closing the door behind him and turned to Tam. "How are you feeling honey?"

"Sore- and you?"

"Sore." lying down next to her, Gabe smiled when she took his hand and squeezed.

"Your doctor should be in shortly. They won't answer any of my questions and are really starting to piss me off."

"I know they came in several times after you scolded that nurse out of here to check my vitals."

"Can you move your toes?"

"And my leg. It's sore and hurts, so I guess that's good."

Gabe leaned over, his lips gently brushing across hers. "It is, and you get to put up with me while we heal. Kline has put me on house rest as long as it's with you."

"I thought you said you were grazed."

Gabe shrugged. "A graze; shot straight through, I'm fine."

"Gabe!"

Gabe met her gaze as she leaned away. "I'm fine. It was a clean shot. I've had worse. It didn't hit anything vital, no nerve damage, all that good stuff." When she opened her mouth to argue with him, he rolled, his mouth covering hers. He slowly slid his tongue along her lip, dipping in. His ears perked as someone cleared their throat. "Go away, I'm giving mouth-to-mouth."

Tam smacked his arm as he rolled away to see Zack half-way in the room. "Well?"

"We have a perp."

Gabe's gaze didn't leave his brother's as he walked to stand at the end of their beds.

"Vivian Robinson."

"Who is?"

"Remember how Caitlin said her ex started making threats against Tam?"

"Yeah."

"Her fingerprints are all over that car. The owner said she had just met Vivian two months ago at a club downtown. They've hung out a couple times, but she noticed something off about Ms. Robinson and tried to distance herself. She had no idea her car had been gone, never mind used in the drive by. She works nights and was sleeping. When patrol got there, she was still in bed."

"Where's the perp now?"

"We're looking. We have an APB out and four teams hitting the pavement, I've also given photos to all hospital employees to be on the lookout, while you two are here."

"What about Caitlin? Has someone warned her?" Tam asked.

"Yes, Marc went over this morning and had a talk with her. She's been very helpful."

~~*~~

"What the hell do you mean, you haven't found her yet?" Gabe growled. "It's been a fucking week."

"I know," Zack said as he moved to sit on the couch. "We almost had her two days ago, she has no social media that we can find, her job said she quit the day you two were shot, and she hasn't used her cell, bank, or credit cards."

Gabe's gaze narrowed. "And?"

"I was thinking of flushing her out."

"How?" When Zack glanced up and met his gaze, Gabe's eyes widened. "Oh, fuck no, little brother. Don't even think it."

"Think what?" Tamara asked as they continued to stare each other down.

"He wants to use you as bait, to lure her out. And it's not fucking happening."

"Gabe, stop swearing. Zack, is this true?"

"Yeah, I hate to say it, but yeah." Zack answered.

"It's not happening!" Gabe snapped. "I am not putting

her in the line of fire again!" His fist slammed down on the counter top.

"It will be in a controlled environment, Gabe."

"There is no such thing. There are too many variables where things can go wrong!"

"Gabe," Tam said.

Gabe met her gaze. "I said no," he snarled.

When Zack stood, Gabe stepped forward, fists clenching. "You saw damn well how great the controlled environment went with Syd. She got stabbed. I am not putting Tam in that situation!"

"Unfortunately, it's not up to you. Kline's already okayed it if Tamara agrees."

"Not happening!"

"Not up to you!"

Gabe went toe-to-toe with Zack, nostrils flaring. "Don't fucking push me on this!"

"Stop it!" Tamara grabbed Gabe's arm. "Just stop. Zack, maybe you should go for now…"

"How about for the rest of the fucking case!"

"Gabriel! I said stop."

Gabe moved his gaze to her.

"What the hell is going on? I can hear the yelling down in the bar." Walt said as he ran in.

"Don't ask." Tam said. "Just take Zack with you, before they come to blows."

Gabe's chest heaved. How in the hell could Zack even think to toss Tam into the fire? What the hell was he thinking, especially after Sydney got stabbed while closing the case down? Hell, Zack had almost lost his mind when he turned and saw the knife sticking out of her side. Glancing down when he felt pressure on his chest, he noticed Tamara's small hand resting there. "Tam."

"Gabe, I know what you're going to say. Let's just shove it aside for tonight. Calm down and then we can talk."

"Are you saying you want to do this?"

"I'm saying, we need to be a bit calmer before we talk about if it happens."

"Don't fucking placate me. If you've already made up your mind to do it, just say so."

"I haven't made up my mind to do anything and so help me, if you swear at me again, I'll smack some sense into you, Gabriel Mac Cloud! I said we were going to calm down first, and damn it, don't you get me upset!"

Gabe's gaze followed her as she limped over to the barstool. Glancing at the floor for a moment, he lifted his gaze back to her as she slid her bottom onto the wooden chair and stepped over to her, wrapping his arms around her as she laid her head on his chest. He touched his chin to the top of her head. "I don't want you hurt. I couldn't stop you from getting shot, I'm not going to put you in a situation where the probability of you getting hurt is more than fifty percent. There's no way Tam, I can't let that happen." Tightening his arms around her, his chest rose with a heavy sigh. Her fingers made small movements on his back, taking away his aggression. Lowering his head, he found her lips, softly, soulfully loving her, his hands moved up to cradle her neck, his fingers weaving through her hair as he claimed her mouth with his.

Gabe moved his hands down her arms to her back and lifted her against him, one hand on her ass, the other at her back as she wove her arms around his neck, their mouths never breaking from each other. Swinging her up into his arms, he carried her to the bedroom. Kicking the door shut with his foot, he sat her gently on the mattress. "Are you well enough for this?"

"Yes."

Her breathless reply had his cock hard almost to the point of pain. Bringing her up to the middle of the bed, his mouth lowered to her neck as he settled himself between her thighs, laying there, he felt her legs come up on his sides.

"Gabe."

"Hmmm?"

"Get naked."

"In time."

"No, now."

Gabe lifted his head to meet her gaze.

"I want to feel you against me, please."

His brow lifted. "Seeing as how you asked so nicely." Sitting back on his knees, she came up a bit with him.

She drew his shirt up, her hand caressed his stomach, causing his muscles to quiver.

"It may not be as slow as we need to take it, sweetheart."

"That's ok, I just need to feel you."

Gabe smiled, she was a sensory, she was tactile. She liked feeling and touching. He liked that, but when they had time and weren't recovering from bullet wounds, he'd have to teach her to wait. When he tossed the shirt and looked down at her, she was removing her own. Gabe zeroed in and went straight to her nipples, sucking and biting until she cried and wiggled with pleasure.

And then he was between her thighs. God, he loved the taste of her. Flicking his tongue out, he hit her clit, then nibbled. Her thighs moved close to his head, her fingers in his hair and grabbing her breasts as passion radiated through her body.

When she was close, he stopped, quickly moving, and slid his rigidness against her clit, his gaze on her as she trembled, his name on her lips.

Her hand grabbed his forearm as he sank into her slowly. She arched against him with a sigh on her lips.

"My God baby." He groaned, covering the whole of her body with his.

"Oh my God Gabe, you feel so good."

Gabe grinned and began to move, her parted lips an invitation and landed his mouth on hers, her pussy pulsed around him, so hot and wet. God, he'd been waiting for her for so long. Careful of her thigh, he moved slightly to her other side, taking the pressure off.

Her nails scrapped down his back and the fire took off between them. He increased his thrusts, his mouth going to the crook of her neck, biting and growled when she nipped his shoulder. Something cracked open inside him as they pleasured each other, driving deep. She arched, crying out his name, her fingers digging into his flesh, trembling against him as her walls convulsed. Gabe fisted his hands in her hair, groaning her name as he followed her over.

CHAPTER 7

TAMARA'S GAZE SWUNG TO GABE as he growled at Zack over the desk, the moment using her for bait was mentioned. Captain Kline had called them in. "Gabe, let's hear them out." Gabe's gaze cut to her, sharp and scowling. "Go ahead Captain." She knew his gaze narrowed as she turned her attention to Kline.

"We want to have you drive your car out of here back to the bar. Gabe will be following you on his bike."

"But didn't she bug my car?"

"Yes. We want to nab her at the Merfay. It's the perfect place, you'll be surrounded by undercovers and off duty cops, not to mention the ones in on this sting."

"There's only one way in or out for her." Zack said. "She doesn't have the key for the backdoor and we have cameras hidden everywhere, so we'll know when she appears."

"You don't have to leave her side." Kline said.

"Obviously, I do," Gabe snapped. "How in the hell else are we going to lure her close enough to Tam to get what we need?"

Tam held up her hand when Kline and Zack went to chime in. "Gentlemen, if you'd give us a moment please." Tam met Gabe's gaze, took his hand in hers. "Gabe look at me." His jaw clenched. "Gabe…"

"No, Tam!"

Laying her hand on his chest, she waited until he calmed. "Please listen to me. I want this over, Gabe. I want to get on with my life, my job, you. I don't want to be stuck in a safe house. I want us to live and explore what we've found."

"Baby, I don't want you getting hurt."

"I know. Trust me, I know. Every time you went out, I could see you leaving on your Harley from my office. My stomach dropped because I knew you were going out on a case and potential danger. You're a cop. Every time you leave, your life is in danger. You got shot, Gabe. Because of me, you got shot. I couldn't stop that." Her eyes glazed over as she shook her head slightly and he finally turned to meet her gaze

Gabe grabbed her into his embrace and Tam clung to him. "I understand, Gabe. I really do. I'll gear up, wear a vest, whatever you want. I just want this over with."

"I've never seen him like this, you know." Zack said.

Tam followed him down to the garage. "Grumbly and bear-like?" she chuckled.

"In love."

Tam stopped. Her gaze met his as he turned. "I, um…"

"It's okay, Tamara. It's good for him, good for the both of you."

Love? Was it even possible in such a short amount of time? Yeah, she'd admired him from afar, as he did her, but – Tam smiled.

"Besides, you're the only person I know who can calm him down before or in the middle of an angry rant."

"Not always." She said, thinking back to when they

were locked in the stock room. Then again, he did calm down as they talked. Smiling when Zack glanced at her, Tam walked over to her car.

"The bug's been put back where we found it. It's GPS only, no audio or visual, and should ping her the moment you set the car in motion. Have you ever fired a weapon?"

"A gun, no."

"Shit, I didn't think of that. I was going to put one by the door on the inside, easily reachable in case you need it. We'll switch it out for a taser."

"Well, Gabe will be right behind me, right?"

"Yeah, yeah, he's already waiting for you and we have two more officers that will be following you at a distance, and switching off with two more along the route back to the bar. You'll be covered at all times and Gabe will get you suited after you get there."

Tam's chest rose with a deep breath. "Okay. I can do this." Nodding her head when he opened the door, she took a seat and started the car.

"Tam."

"Yeah?"

"It'll be all right."

"Yeah."

"Here, put this in."

Tam took the ear bud and set it in her ear. "Gabe?"

"Right here, baby." Gabe replied.

Tam kept an eye out as she headed back to the bar. Gabe was in her rearview mirror all the way and in her ear, speaking to her and keeping her calm. Parking on the side of the bar, she got out as he parked next to her, stepping up when he got off, she leaned into him as he wrapped an arm around her waist and then headed in.

Tam glanced down at his dark head as he fit the vest to her. She hadn't seen this kind of vest before. It fit her better than the others she'd worn; he said they'd borrowed it from SWAT's only female member. He was connecting her mic to the vest. It was so small. The technology nowadays was amazing. "Is that thing live?"

"Not yet."

Her nostrils flared, nipples grazing the inside of her bra. "Gabe, I like you."

"I like you too baby."

She glanced at his head. "No, I mean, I --" His warm knuckles grazed her side.

"Yeah honey, me too."

"Shit Gabe," Tam palmed his cheeks in her hands and had him look up to meet her gaze. "Gabe, I'm trying to tell you, I love you."

Gabe smiled as he kissed the inside of her palm. His hands lay on her hips as he stood.

Tam met his mouth hungrily.

"I love you too, baby." He whispered. "So, you two morons hearing this, know if anything happens to her, I'll string you up by your toes."

Tam's head went back as she met his gaze.

"Yeah, we're live now."

"Tam, try to act normal, honey. You're supposed to be having a good time out drinking and playing pool. Maybe you should have a drink to settle your nerves."

"I don't think that's a good idea." Tam said as she leaned into his warmth.

"One drink is not going to inebriate you."

"Fine." Walking over to the bar, Tam smiled as

Walt headed her way. "Can I have a cranberry juice and vodka?"

"Sure, what kind of vodka?"

"That one's fine." Tam smiled as Walt mixed her drink then handed it to her and she headed back to the pool table. She was halfway through and just finished a game when Gabe came up behind her, his arm wrapped around her waist dragging her close to his strong body, and she leaned back on him, letting him support her weight.

"You're calmer." He whispered in her ear.

"Mmm." Damn, she loved being close to him, his scent, touch, everything. Laying her head back against his shoulder, her gaze scanned the crowd and she tensed.

"I know, she came in about five minutes ago." He whispered as he kissed the side of her neck.

"What do we do?" Her whispered words were barely heard above her heartbeat.

"Act normal." His lips touched the side of her neck. "I need you to calm down."

"Okay."

"Don't look at her, I want you to look at Marc."

"Why?"

"Don't ask questions. Do as I tell you."

The sharpness of his tone had her gaze swinging to Marc, who smiled at them. Damn ear buds. They wouldn't give her one, because they didn't want her to worry if she heard something, like when Vivian was sighted outside. She didn't need his cousin and brothers to know she obeyed him, because then they'd guess she did when they were intimate. Tam frowned. Then again, they probably knew he was as Alpha as they come and what he liked.

"Why are you frowning?"

"Tell Marc to stop smiling at me, he's creeping me out, the perv." Her gaze whipped over to Zack when he busted out laughing.

"I think you just did, baby." Gabe chuckled. "Now lean back again and shut your eyes."

Tam's chest rose, her breasts rubbed against the metal vest as she listened to his voice, his whispering. She hoped they couldn't hear on the other end. Her lashes fluttered as she smiled. "Gabe, you're naughty." His wicked chuckle sent shivers through her body, tingles from her scalp to her pussy.

"Breathe deeply in through your nose."

Tam followed his order.

"And out your mouth, slowly – that's my baby. Do you know how sexy you are? I love you in jeans and a t-shirt, your hair half way up and messy looking, like we just jumped out of bed."

The side of Tam's mouth lifted. "You are entirely too sexy, Gabriel Mac Cloud."

"Only for you, baby."

Her body trembled when his lips touched her neck, hers parted with a sigh. "Damn Gabe," she breathed when he ground his hard cock against her butt.

Gabe sucked her earlobe into his mouth, nibbled and released. "I need you to walk to the ladies' room. Catia is there and ready. Breathe and stay calm. The moment she follows you, we'll be at the door."

Tam opened her eyes slowly, her gaze going to the small hall where the restrooms were. Breathing deeply. No, problem, she could do this. She wasn't alone. Gabe and his brothers were right here with a ton of other cops and Catia was in the bathroom just in case. Her hand shook as she went forward, turned and met his gaze. "I need to go to the ladies' room." Leaning in, she brushed her lips against his. "I'll be right back."

Gabe winked. "I'll be waiting."

Tam smiled, brow arched, then glanced down. "Oh, I'm sure you will."

Gabe smacked her ass, grinned and gripped. "Hurry up baby, let's wrap up this game and scoot, hitting the rack early tonight sounds like a plan."

"Hmmmm." Smiling she turned and headed to the ladies' room. Ok, this would be over tonight, she had backup all around her, and she wanted to do this. The plan sounded good as they went over it, but she hadn't figured in her nerves. Damn, she could do this. She was wired and had the vest on. "Okay." Blowing out a breath she winked at Jake as she entered the hallway.

Coming out of the stall, she flushed the toilet. No one had entered while she faked going to the bathroom. She walked to the sink, the warm water flowed over her hands as the lather bubbled. Maybe Vivian wouldn't approach her, maybe all this was for nothing, but she knew one thing, Vivian wouldn't be getting out of the bar without handcuffs on. Turning when the door opened, she held her breath as Vivian walked in and stared at her. Smiling softly, Tam went back to washing her hands.

"You've got a good-looking man there, if I was into men, that is." Vivian said.

"Huh, oh thank you."

"Been together long?"

"No, not really, but we've been flirting with it for a couple of years. It just happened naturally, I guess."

Grabbing some paper towels, she twisted them around her hands.

"Uh-huh, or maybe because he was made to watch over you?"

Tam frowned. "I'm sorry?"

"You're such a fucking whore."

Tam stepped toward the door, only to be blocked by Vivian. "Excuse me."

"Nope."

"I'm trying to leave. Please let me by."

"I don't think so."

Tam backed up when she saw the glint of a knife. "Do I know you?"

"No, but I know you. You know, you might be hot to look at and watch in bed, but you're really nothing but a whore and it's all your fault."

"What is?" Tam asked, keeping the conversation going to see if she could get a confession out of Vivian. "Are you, are you the one who's been threatening me?"

Vivian laughed sarcastically. "Yeah, and the one who shot you. If it wasn't for you, she'd still be with me!"

Tam backed up when she waved the knife around. "Who'd still be with you? I don't understand."

"Caitlin, you stupid bitch! Because of you, she left me. Because of you, she wants nothing to do with me!"

"Caitlin, Caitlin from the office?"

"Yes! Caitlin from your office. My God, you're a stupid one! She left me because of you!"

"What do I have to do with it? As you can see I'm into men, not women."

"Because she had a crush on you. All she did was talk about you, what Tamara wore, how your hair looked, what purse you had, your car, your- she even bought a damn wig to look like you! Tamara this, Tamara that! When I told her to shut the hell up or I'd kill you, she left me!"

"I'm sorry, but I had nothing to do with that. I had no idea Caitlin liked women or she had a crush on me."

"Then why would you smile at her every morning, every time you walked to the D.A.'s office?"

"Because it's being courteous to fellow workers. To smile and say good morning. Are you really the one who tried to kill me? Did you hire that guy from the store?"

"Of course, I did! And once I get rid of you, I'm going to take care of Caitlin, the little tramp. I'll slice her like I'm gonna do to you."

Tamara backed up.

"What do you think that cop is gonna do when he finds you bleeding out all over the floor?"

"He'll come after you," Tam breathed softly. "If you hurt me, he won't stop until he has you." *Stay calm, they're right out side the door and Catia is watching them from the other stall.*

"Then maybe I'll have to kill him too."

"I'll scream."

Vivian laughed. "Go ahead. Do you think anyone will hear you over that music? Dumbass."

"You don't have to do this. You haven't hurt me yet. If you do, you'll be up for a felony. That could mean prison for the rest of your life."

"Don't be stupid!"

Tam screeched and moved to the side as Vivian came at her. It all happened so fast. The blade stuck her front and side, but the vest reflected it as Catia burst out of the stall, grabbed Vivian's hand and shoved her back against the sink.

"Catia! Look ou…" Catia lost her grip on the hand with the knife and Tam grabbed it, struggling with Vivian. "Gabe!" Catia was able to toss Vivian to the floor as the door busted open, Tam went down with them, not letting go of Vivian's hand and pressed her knee to the side of Vivian's head as Gabe and Zack rushed in.

"Get off me, you bitch!" Vivian yelled. "I'll fucking kill you!"

Tam watched Gabe grab the knife. He had to wrestle it out of her hand as Zack helped Catia handcuff Vivian, before she came up.

"Are you all right?" Gabe asked.

"Yeah." Glancing down, she saw where the knife had cut through her shirt to the vest below. "Catia got hit."

"Yeah, she's going to need stitches." Jake said.

Tam wrapped her arms around Gabe when he stepped over to her, handing the knife off to Marc.

"I'm going to kill all of you!" Vivian snarled. "Police brutality, you bastard. I'll have your job!"

"Body cameras. I haven't touched you." Gabe said. "Marc, get her the hell out of here."

Tam kept her gaze on the screaming woman as Marc and John hauled her out of the bathroom. Jake shoved a towel on Catia's arm before leading her out to a waiting ambulance. Glancing up at Gabe, she breathed a shaky sigh.

"Are you all right?"

"I think so."

"You'll be coming off the adrenaline rush. You may get sick. Let's get you upstairs, baby."

Tam let out a little chuckle. "Hang on to me so I don't fall. My knees are like jelly."

Gabe

"Yeah, well for jelly, you jumped in awful quick to help Catia out."

"My dad made sure we knew how to defend ourselves, but you never know how you'll act until you have no other choice. I'm glad I didn't freeze up."

"Me too, sweetheart." He kissed the top of her head.

Tam noticed how the bar buzzed with conversation. If she didn't know better, she'd say nothing happened in here, they all looked like they had before she went into the bathroom. Then again, that's what these guys and girls did, undercover work and they were good at it.

CHAPTER 8

TAMARA GLANCED DOWN AT GABE'S head. He was removing the mic and vest.

"I'm glad you had this on."

"Me too," she murmured, as he ran his fingers across the open slash in her t-shirt. "Gabe?"

"Yeah."

"Is that thing off?"

"Yeah, I disconnected it."

Her hands went to the sides of his face, cupping his cheeks and added pressure until he met her gaze. "I really have fallen for you, Gabriel Mac Cloud. Don't break my heart."

Gabe stood. "That's the last thing I'd ever want to do."

Tam stood on tiptoes when he lowered his head and met his lips with hers. His arms wrapped around her waist, drawing her close. The heat of his body radiated through her clothing, sending tremors through her body.

Tam twitched when the door opened.

"Hey, you two coming down for a drink?" Zack asked.

Gabe smirked. "No, we're going to have incredibly passionate sex, so get out."

Tam chuckled as Gabe lifted her into his arms. "Lock the door behind you, Zack!" Wrapping her arm around

Gabe

Gabe's neck, she kissed the underside of his jaw as he kicked the bedroom door shut.

A PEEK INSIDE JAKE

Jake frowned, feet braced apart, arms crossed over his chest. Who in the hell did this bike belong to? Walking around the 2017 Suzuki GW250, he knew they had to be a cop and a female at that. Every morning for the past two months, this bike and its driver would mess with him on his way into the station.

"What are you doing, shopping for a new look?" Gabe asked as he strolled in.

"It's this bike, man. This is the one I've been telling you about, the one that fucks with me every morning."

Jake turned at Gabe's chuckle. "What's so funny?"

"You moron and the fact you can't figure out who rides it." Gabe slapped him on the shoulder as he took off for the stairs. "Let's go, Columbo. We've got work to do."

Jake flung one last scowl at the terrorizer before following his brother.

JAKE – Undercover Lover Series Book III - Releasing November 17, 2018

ABOUT THE AUTHOR

Ms. Salo, is a current member of RWA (https://www.rwa.org/)and reached RWA's PRO status in April of 2015. Ms. Salo, is serving as the Vice President of Communications for the 2018-19 term, and served as the Interim Vice President of Programs for her RWA chapter, The Sunshine State Romance Authors for the 2017 year.

C.A. is originally from north central Massachusetts, and moved down to central Florida where she swears she hates shoveling as much as humidity.
C and her Hubs tied the knot during an intimate ceremony on her Grandmother's birthday in March at a beautiful and charming B & B in Fl.

Blog: http://authorcasalo.blogspot.com/
Facebook: https://www.facebook.com/authorcasalo
Twitter: https://twitter.com/AuthorCASalo

Website: http://www.authorcasalo.com